Stop That Dog!

Written by Peter Bently

Illustrated by Steve May

The Sharma family was at the funfair.

"Can we watch the puppet show?" asked Ana.

"But Puff and I want to go to the dog races!" grumbled Arun.

"Let's split up," said Dad. "Arun and Puff can come with me while Mum takes the girls to see the puppets."

Ana and Asha enjoyed the puppets and giggled a lot. When the show had finished, they spoke to the puppet man.

"That was really funny!" said Ana.
"I'm glad you enjoyed it," smiled
the puppet man. "Now I'm off for
my lunch."

Suddenly Arun and Dad ran up, out of breath.

"Did Puff win the race?" asked Mum.

"No," panted Arun. "When it started, he ran in the wrong direction. Now we've lost him!"

"Don't worry," said Mum. "He can't have gone far."

"Look!" said Ana. "There he is! After him!"

But Puff was zipping along like a rocket and they couldn't catch him. He jumped over a bookstall, knocking most of the books to the ground.

"What a mess!" moaned the woman on the stall.

"Sorry!" said Dad. "I'll put everything back."

"Let's follow Puff," said Mum.

They chased Puff into the tea tent.
"Look out!" exclaimed a man carrying
a large cake.

But it was too late. Puff ran right into him. Cream and jam went everywhere.
Asha giggled, but the man was furious.
"I'm so sorry," Mum said. "I'll pay for the cake."

Arun chased Puff onto the helter skelter. "I've cornered him now!" he thought, as he reached the top of the steps.

But before
Arun could grab
him, Puff zoomed
down the slide and
ran off.

"He's heading that
way!" Arun cried.

At the barbecue they heard someone shouting.

"It's the puppet man," said Ana. "What's Puff done now?"

"He's got something in his mouth," said
Arun.

"Stop that dog!" wailed the puppet man.
"He's stolen half my chicken burger!"

Finally, Dad grabbed Puff's collar.

"Got you!" he cried.

"What about my chicken burger?" complained the puppet man. "I can't eat it now."

"We'll buy you another one," said Mum.

"The burgers look delicious," said Dad. "Who else would like one?"

"Me!" replied Arun and Asha together.

Dad bought chicken burgers for everyone.
While they were eating, they heard an
announcement:
   "The next dog race
is about to start!"

"Come on," said Arun. "Let's take Puff."

"But what if he escapes again?" asked Mum.

"Don't worry," said Arun. "I've got an idea!"

They got to the start line just in time. Ana waited there with Puff while Arun went to the end of the racetrack.

"Where are you going?" asked Dad.

"I'm making sure Puff doesn't run in the wrong direction," replied Arun.

"But how?" asked Mum.
"Wait and see!" grinned Arun.

The announcer started the race. "Ready? Get set! Go!"

Mum, Dad and Ana cheered as Puff ran off down the track.

Puff zipped past the other dogs, sped over the finish line and ran straight up to Arun.

"He won!" cheered Ana. "Hooray!"

All the other dogs followed Puff.
Arun disappeared under a heap of
fur and wagging tails!

"Well done, Arun!" smiled Mum. "But how did you make Puff run towards you?"

"Simple," beamed Arun. "I saved some of my chicken burger. Puff ran straight for it! But I forgot that all the other dogs would want some too!"

"What a very clever idea!" laughed Dad. "Well done, both of you!"